10/06

D1509947

I 5 11/11

my amazon river day

By Kris Nesbitt
Photography by Edward G. Lines Jr.

Shedd Aquarium
Chicago

Shedd
The World's Aquarium

Shedd Aquarium
1200 S. Lake Shore Drive
Chicago, Illinois 60605
www.sheddaquarium.org

Copyright © 2000 Shedd
Aquarium. All rights reserved.
No part of this book may be
reproduced without permission
from the publisher. Printed in the
United States of America.

Janet E. Powers
  Project director
Karen Furnweger
  Editor
Jennifer Bennett
  Art director
Jeni Moore
  Graphic designer
Sally Smith
  Illustrator
Carrie Stickan
  Illustrator
Laura Jenkins
  Children's literature consultant

Library of Congress Cataloging-in-Publication Data
Nesbitt, Kris
  My Amazon River Day/by Kris Nesbitt.
  48 p. cm.
  Includes bibliographical information.
  Summary: Details a day in the life of
  Amazon children.
  1. Amazon River – Juvenile. 2. Sustainable
development – Amazon River Valley – Juvenile
literature. 3. Anthropology – Amazon River
Valley. 4. Amazon River – ethnobotany. I. Title.
  QH112.N458
  577.098
  ISBN 0-9701035-0-6

Additional photo credits
p. 5 left, Patrice Ceisel; p. 27 bottom,
Kris Nesbitt; p. 28 lower right,
James L. Castner; p. 45, Devon Graham

Our warm thanks and deep appreciation go to the entire Shahuano family, who generously and graciously welcomed us into their home; to the three Shahuano children – Patricia, José and Eriberto – who patiently shared their daily lives with us; to the schoolteachers – Isaac Sinojara Tello, Mildred Flores Paredes and Marili Vàsquez Peña – and the children of the Apayacu school; to the children and families of Apayacu; to César Peña Bardeles, our guide and translator, who helped with our understanding of the family's activities; to Devon Graham, Ph.D., our content advisor and logistics coordinator; to Fernando Rios and the Margarita Tours boat crew; to traveling companions Patrice Ceisel, Jim Morrissette and Barbara Becker; to Pat Platt and Meg Bross, who provided valuable feedback on early drafts; and to Connie Nesbitt and her students at West Chester Friends School, for their initial inspiration and help along the way.

Nelber
NEHL bair

Jovita
hoh BEE tah

Berto
BAIR toh

Papi
pah PEE

Mami
mah MEE

Rosana
roh ZAH nah

José
hoh SAY

Patricia
pah TREE see ah

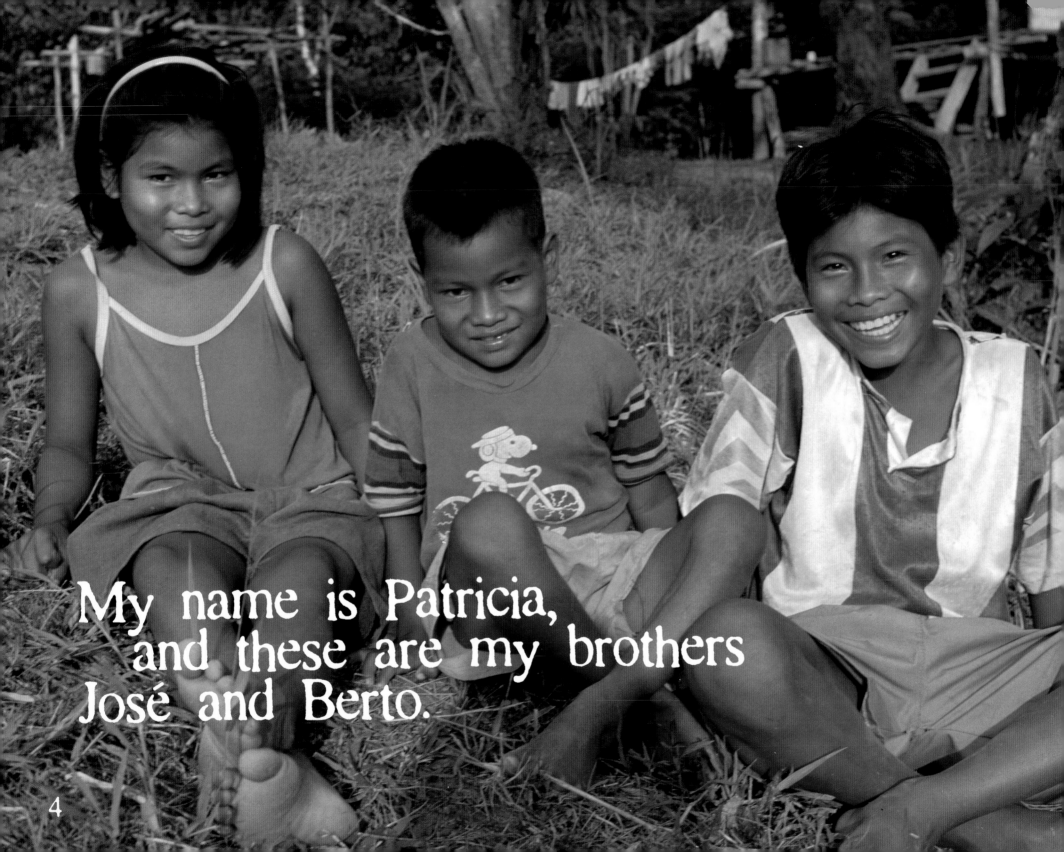

My name is Patricia,
and these are my brothers
José and Berto.

4

I am 10, José is 8, and Berto is 13. We live in Peru with our parents. Our big sister, Rosana, her husband, Nelber, and their daughter, Jovita, live with us, too. Our house stands on a bank above a small river that meets the Amazon River. We are ribereños. That means "people who live near the river" in Spanish, the language we speak.

This is our house and our dog, Duquesa. Sometimes Duquesa acts like she's the queen of the house. But we know better. Mami and Papi are really in charge.

ribereños (ree beh REN yohs)

Duquesa (doo KAY sah): this is "Duchess" in Spanish

5

Our neighborhood changes during the year. The level of the river rises and falls, depending on the season. Rainy season comes, and the water begins to rise. In high-water season, the river floods the forest for a few months and surrounds our house up to the floorboards.

Now it's low-water season. We have to climb down a tall bank to get to the water. The river is very important to us. It's where we get many of the things we need. We catch fish to eat in the river, and we take our canoes to market on it.

water level

What's life like for José, Berto and me?
Come spend a day with us.
It's the middle of October,
        during low-water season.

7

I wake up
    to the sound
of birds calling loudly.

Before dawn, the many birds of the forest begin to chirp and call, and it sounds like music. I lie in bed and listen to the birds. When the roosters in our neighborhood start crowing, I know it's time to get up. I share a tent of mosquito netting with José. The tent keeps bugs from biting us in the night. Some mornings I have to tickle José to wake him up. But today we both get up quickly and put away our tent.

My brothers and I do chores in the morning before school. The first chore is getting water from the river for cooking and washing. Today Berto gets water while Mami, Rosana and I make breakfast. We light a fire in the hearth, which is in the corner and raised off the floor. Rosana makes mazamorra, a porridge of corn and plantain flour.

mazamorra (mah zah MOR ah)

plantain (plan TAYN): a starchy fruit that looks like a banana

9

While we cook, José goes to the river. Every night, he strings a net across a creek that runs into the river near our house. Every morning, he paddles there in our canoe to see if he caught any fish. He brings them home in a bucket. Today, he caught a lot of fish! We'll eat them for dinner.

This morning, Papi works on a new canoe that he's making out of a log from the forest. Over the last week, he burned and carved out the shape of the canoe. Now he's stretching it out with smaller pieces of wood. José likes to help him find the right nails for the job.

After breakfast, we take our dirty clothes and dishes to the river to wash them. When the water is high, we can do it right off the porch. We scrub the clothes and dishes. Then we climb the bank to hang the laundry or lay it on the ground to dry in the sun. If it's really humid, the laundry can take a few days to dry.

After breakfast and morning chores, Mami and Papi get in our big canoe and head off to our farm fields, where we grow yuca, corn and beans during low-water season. Every year the floods leave lots of mud behind in the forest. The new mud makes the soil good for growing crops. The farm fields my parents cleared from the forest are a little far from our house. Sometimes Mami and Papi don't come home until the afternoon.

Rosana stays home with Jovita during the day. Today Rosana reminds us to feed the chickens. Berto gets some rice, and we call "coo-coo." Soon the chickens are at our feet gobbling up the rice. The chickens live under our house during low-water season. When the water is high, we bring them onto the porch so they don't get wet.

yuca (YOO kuh): a root that tastes like a potato

We live next-door
to our school.

16

During low-water season we walk to school. But most of our
village is across the river, and the kids and teachers come to
school in a big boat. Some kids paddle to school in their own canoes.
In high-water season, we take a canoe, too.

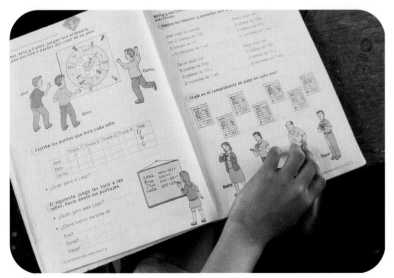

I like our school. There are two classrooms and three classes. José and I are in the room with the youngest kids, first through third grades. Our teacher is Señor Sinojara.

Berto is in the other classroom. His teacher, Señora Flores, is really nice. She'll be my teacher next year. The oldest kids sit in the back of Berto's room and have another teacher. Our school is for kids up to age 14 or 15. After that, we either stop going to school or go away to high school in a bigger village, like my oldest brother does. We go to school most of the year, except for three months starting in December, when floodwaters are getting high. Like our house, school is built on stilts to keep it dry.

Señor Sinojara (sehn YOR SEE noh HAHR ah)

Señora Flores (sehn YOR ah FLOW res)

We start the day by raising the flag of Peru and singing our national anthem. While we sing, the helper for the day sweeps the room. During the day, the helper has to get water from the river for us to drink. After we raise the flag, we start class.

School can be hard, especially when Señor Sinojara calls us up to the blackboard to answer a question. He calls on José today. In school, we learn mathematics, reading, writing, spelling, health, history, science and geography. Mathematics is my favorite, but I also like singing in class. José's favorite subject is recess.

In Berto's class, they study the same things, only they're harder. Berto is a good student, but I hear that sometimes he gets in trouble for whispering to his friends.

In the middle of our school day, we get half an hour of recess. Usually the boys play soccer, and the girls play volleyball. Sometimes kids run around chasing each other. When Señora Flores rings the school bell, we go back to class.

23

After school,
everybody heads home.

24

School ends around 1 o'clock. Mami and Papi are still at our fields, but Rosana is home. She says it's time to start making our big meal of the day. But first we have a snack. Today, Jovita was playing with a watermelon like it was a ball, and it rolled off the porch and broke. That means that we get to eat it now! Then I light the fire in our hearth so we can cook.

Berto goes to our garden to get some yuca roots. First he pulls up a plant, then he cuts the roots off with a machete, a large, wide knife. Yuca is an important crop for us. We eat some kinds of yuca roots fried or boiled. Other kinds have to be grated and baked into flour, or they can make you sick. We make bread and pancakes with the flour.

Today we are going to boil the yuca roots Berto cut and eat them with fish. I peel the roots with a machete and then put them in a pot. While we were at school, Nelber caught three piranhas for us to eat with the fish that José caught in his net.

machete (mah CHEH teh)

piranha (pih RAHN yah)

26

Berto goes out in his canoe to spear more fish. Spearing fish is hard. José and I are still trying to learn. Berto and Papi are trying to teach us how to see fish underwater and time our throws right. José would rather paddle around or chase other kids in canoes. During high-water season, we like to paddle into the flooded forest. There we see side-necked turtles and caiman lizards swimming in the water.

caiman (CAY mehn) lizard

27

José helps Rosana and me while we cook. His job is to fan the smoke away from the fire. When Berto gets back from fishing, he and José play soccer. Then they climb a tree. José follows Berto high up the tree, but Rosana yells at him to climb down. José is too little to climb that high.

José is good at climbing shorter trees in the forest to collect fruit. He's learning how to use a machete to cut the fruit off. One time he cut himself. He came running home, but Mami took him back into the forest to a sangre del grado tree. She slit its bark, and red sap oozed out. Then she put the sap on his cut. It got better really fast. That sap helps bad insect bites heal, too.

sangre del grado (SAHN greh del GRAH doh)

28

We'll wait
to eat until our
parents come home.

efore we eat, I like to rest or play in the hammock with Jovita. I watch Duquesa, too. Sometimes José climbs in the rafters of our house. The palm thatch roof is woven tight to keep out rain. Our house is made of woods and plants from the forest. We use palm twine to hold logs together. For the stilts of our house, we use hardwood that won't rot even when the river is up to our floorboards. Even our hammock comes from the forest. Mami wove it from palm twine pulled from young palm leaves.

When I hear Berto yell that our parents are here, I run to see what they've brought home. Sometimes their canoe is full of yuca or beans. Today Mami found palm fruits in the forest. She'll boil them to make a drink. Papi caught some catfish. We eat lots of fish!

Before I know it, we're eating. I'm hungry today! We did a good job cooking. The fish José caught with his net taste good. And so does the yuca Berto cut.

After we eat, Berto, José and I get our toothbrushes and brush our teeth. We learned in school how important it is to brush every day.

Papi rests in the hammock. Mami likes to keep things neat, so she uses a machete to cut away weeds growing in the yard. Berto has a good idea — he thinks we should go to the village to see our friends. We ask Mami if it's okay, then we get in our canoe.

We learned how to canoe when we were 4 or 5 years old. Pretty soon Jovita will be old enough to learn! She already loves to ride in the canoe. When we get to the village, Berto pulls the canoe up to the bank and climbs out. He stabs the canoe paddle's pointy head into the ground and ties up the canoe so it won't float away.

A lot of people are in the village today because the boat from Iquitos, the big city, just left. People on this boat buy the crops we harvest to sell at the city market. Sometimes we buy supplies from that boat. Other times we get what we need from a store that floats on a raft at the village. Today Mami gave me money to buy sugar from the raft store.

While I get sugar, Berto finds some friends and starts a soccer game. Berto is good at soccer, and his team usually wins. José thinks he's really good, too. But he's not as good as he thinks he is.

Today, José sits out for a lot of the game. He plays with his friend Raul. Raul has a ron-ron, a toy we make with a flattened bottle cap and a piece of string. If you spin a ron-ron, it goes "whrrr-whrr."

It's getting late, so I find my brothers, and we paddle home.

ron-ron (rrohn rrohn)

It's time to get
ready for bed.

We take our evening bath in the river. Today José makes us laugh by swimming around in the water like a fish. Then, in the middle of washing his hair, he decides that Duquesa needs a bath, too. He chases her and takes her in the water with him!

The sun begins to set. The forest gets noisy at night. Insects and frogs are calling. José finds a tree frog and plays with it. Sometimes we listen to a soccer game on the radio. Or we relax in the hammocks as the sun goes down. Some nights, Mami makes us a bedtime snack. My favorite is yuca porridge with palm fruits. When it gets dark, we light kerosene lamps.

41

I get pretty sleepy in the evenings. At bedtime, Mami helps us set up our mosquito-net tent. First we put blankets down on the floor, then we put up the netting. After we crawl in, we put more rolled-up blankets along the bottom of the tent to keep mosquitoes out. I hate mosquito bites!

Sometimes José and I whisper to each other before we go to sleep. We tell each other stories about creatures that live in the forest. Our parents tell us stories about spirits that live in trees and protect them from getting chopped down. In the stories, trees can whisper to people. Sometimes José and I pretend that we can hear them. Before we fall asleep, José whispers to me, "Buenos noches!"

ssssssssssssssshhhhhhhhhhhh

n n n n n n buenos noches

43

Peru

Patricia's Village
Iquitos

Amazon River

44

Where Patricia lives

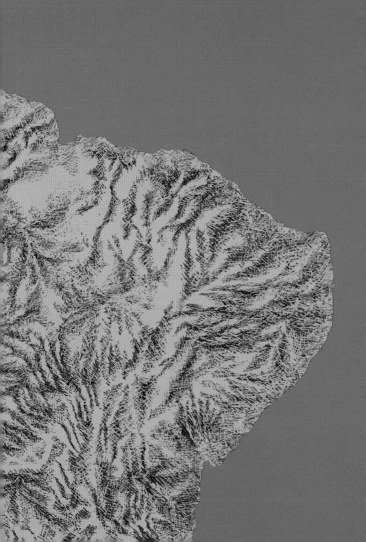

Patricia and her family live near the Amazon River in Peru, a country in South America. The Amazon basin includes the largest river system and rain forest in the world. The Amazon River and its thousand tributaries – smaller rivers that run into it – flow through 9 countries. The river stretches for 3,900 miles, and in some parts it is so wide that you can't see the other side.

The Amazon basin is near the equator, where it is warm all year. The seasons are marked not by changes in temperature but by changes in the level of the river.

At low-water season, rivers and lakes are at their lowest levels, and much of the land is dry.

Next comes the rainy season. It rains a lot in the Amazon – as much as 11 feet a year – and most of the rain falls during the rainy season. Daily downpours raise the Amazon River as much as 6 inches a day. In some parts of the basin, rivers might rise more than 30 feet, touching low-hanging tree branches.

During the high-water season, floodwaters cover many miles of forest on both sides of the river. Fishes swim among the trees looking for fruits, seeds and insects. Families like Patricia and José's canoe right up to their front porches. The water remains high for several months. People who live on the floodplain – called ribereños – know the benefits of the high-water season, and they collect fruits and other food in the flooded forest.

Receding floodwaters sweep fishes back to the river and leave behind rich mud on the forest floor.

Caiman lizards (CAY mehn)

Caiman lizards can be more than 3 feet long. During high-water season, they clamber onto the branches of flooded trees, where they find insects to eat. They also spend a lot of time in the water hunting for snails, shellfish and fishes. Caiman lizards have large, flat teeth that are perfect for crunching hard snail shells. The lizards separate the pieces of shell with their thick tongues and spit them out before swallowing the snail meat.

Catfishes

We know of more than 500 species of catfishes in the Amazon – and more are discovered every year. By comparison, North America has only about 45 species. Amazon catfishes come in all shapes and sizes. Some are shorter than an inch, others are giants 10 feet long. Some species swim almost the whole length of the Amazon River – and back – each year. That's 2,700 miles, the same distance as from New York to Los Angeles!

Fishing in the Amazon

Ribereños have developed many ways to fish in the lakes and rivers of the Amazon floodplain. They use a variety of traps, spears, harpoons, nets and lines, depending on what time of year it is and what fishes they want to catch. Children start learning how to fish when they are about 4 years old.

Flooded forest

Each year during the high-water season, rising rivers flood many miles of Amazon forest. The forest becomes a rich, water-filled habitat that is important to many animals. The trees and other plants are adapted to spending up to six months submerged. Fishes, turtles and other aquatic animals migrate into the flooded forest to feast. Many fishes seek sweet fruits and crunchy nuts that fall from the trees into the water. Others gobble algae and plant debris that grow on tree bark and roots. Insects and spiders that tumble from branches also become meals for animals in the water below.

Floodplain

A floodplain is the land along a river that is underwater part of the year. In the Amazon basin, more than 150,000 square miles flood each year – an area equal to Illinois, Indiana and Wisconsin combined.

Insects

Scientists don't know yet how many different species of insects live in the Amazon, but some guess up to 30 million. Insects are the largest group of animals in the Amazon basin, helping to make the area one of the most biologically diverse places on Earth. Biological diversity means many different kinds of animals and plants. Seventy-two species of ants and 650 species of beetles were found living in one Amazon tree. By comparison, a tree in Illinois might be home to three ant species.

Iquitos, Peru (EE KEE tohs, peh ROO)

Iquitos is the largest city near the area where Patricia and her family live. It's about a daylong boat ride away. Commercial boats stop at smaller towns and villages along the river, like Patricia's, to pick up people and products bound for the city. More than half a million people live in Iquitos, and the population is growing. In some neighborhoods close to the river, homes are raised on stilts so that the yearly floods don't wash them away.

Machete (mah CHEH teh)

A machete is an essential tool on the Amazon floodplain. This large knife with a long, wide blade is used for many chores, including cooking, farming and building. People often take machetes with them on walks into the forest to help clear a path through the vines. Kids learn to use machetes at a young age. Look back in the book to see how many pictures of the family using machetes you can find.

Making a living on the floodplain

An Amazon floodplain neighborhood like the one where Patricia and her family live has three main resources: the river, the forest and farmlands. Ribereños know how to use these resources to grow, harvest and hunt what they need. Rivers and floodplain lakes offer a huge variety of fishes. Fruits, meat and building materials are found in the forest. People grow a wide variety of crops on the new layer of rich, muddy soil that the floods leave behind each year.

Palm trees

More than 22 kinds of palm trees grow on the Amazon floodplain. Ribereños use palm trees in many ways. They eat the fruit, make it into drinks, feed it to livestock and use it as fish bait. Palm twine for hammocks and ropes is pulled from young palm leaves. People weave palm leaves into thatch for roofs. Trunks are cut into planks to build houses. People extract palm oil for cooking and export palm hearts to countries around the world.

Piranhas (pih RAHN yahs)

At least 20 species of piranhas live in the Amazon. They come in many shapes and sizes. Piranhas have a reputation for being vicious, but that's not really the case. Piranhas hardly ever attack large mammals, such as cows, and they don't eat people. (People, however, eat a lot of piranhas, like Patricia's family does.)

Only a few kinds of piranhas gulp whole fish. Some species just nip protein-rich scales and fins from the bodies of other fishes, including other piranhas. Many piranhas eat mostly fruits and nuts. They often find these vegetarian meals in the flooded forest during the high-water season.

Ribereños (ree beh REN yohs)

"Ribereños" is a Spanish word that means "people who live near the river." It is used mostly in Peru to describe people who live in houses, villages and towns along the Amazon floodplain. Most ribereño families have lived on the floodplain for many generations. Their ancestors were Indians, and they also claim European, African and Asian heritage. The way ribereños farm, hunt and fish has developed over many hundreds of years. Their way of life responds to the rise and fall of the Amazon's floods.

Sangre del grado (SAHN greh del GRAH doh)

The Spanish phrase "sangre del grado" means "dragon's blood" in English. Ribereños smear this red tree sap on their skin to soothe insect bites, rashes and wounds, like the one José got with his machete. People also mix it into a drink that can help to heal mouth and stomach ulcers. Dragon's blood is not the only plant that ribereños use as a medicine. They use the bark, sap, leaves and roots of many forest plants as remedies for many illnesses, including infections, flu, indigestion and arthritis. Learning which plants they use may help us develop new medicines. Many medicines that we get at the drugstore were derived from tropical rain forest plants.

Side-necked turtles

Side-necked turtles cannot retract their heads into their shells. Instead, they pull their heads and necks to the side, under the front edge of their shells, for protection. Side-necked turtles often bask on river beaches during the low-water season. They follow rising waters into the flooded forest, eating fruits and seeds that fall into the water.

Soccer

Soccer is one of the most popular activities in the Amazon, played by children and adults alike. A soccer field is often at the center of a community, and many villages have teams that travel by boat to take on other villages' teams on Sundays. Large towns and cities may have teams, too, and their games might be broadcast on the radio.

Tree frogs

Tree frogs have long legs that help them climb among the leaves and branches of trees. Their sticky, round toe pads help them cling to smooth surfaces. Look back at the picture of José holding a tree frog. Can you see the frog's toe pads?

Yuca (YOO kuh)

Yuca is a major food crop in the Amazon. People eat many kinds of thick yuca roots fried or boiled like potatoes, like Patricia's family does. A bitter variety is processed into flour that's used to make bread and pancakes. The tapioca that we use for pudding is a yuca product. You may find yuca in your grocery store. In English, yuca is also called manioc (MAN ee ahk).

47

Make your own ron-ron

José and his friends played with a ron-ron. Here's how to make one yourself. José used a flattened bottle cap to make his ron-ron, but a button or a piece of cardboard works just as well.

What you need
A piece of sturdy, thin string 18 to 20 inches long (like cotton string or fishing line)
A button at least the size of a penny with two holes (or a round piece of heavy cardboard with two holes punched in the middle)

How to make it
Thread the string through one hole in the button or cardboard. Turn that end of the string around and thread it back through the second hole. Tie the two ends of string in a knot. Hold the knot in one hand, and pull the string tight with the other hand. Make sure the button is in the middle. Your ron-ron is finished!

How to make it work
This part is a little harder, but it's fun once you figure it out. Read all the directions before you start. And keep trying! With your palms facing you, slip the ends of the string loop over the first two fingers of each hand. Fold your fingers to tighten your grip on the string. Let the string hang a little. Make sure the button is in the middle of the string. Hold one hand still while you make a fast cranking motion with your other hand. This will twist the string. When the string is twisted tightly, hold both your hands in front of you and, still gripping the string tightly, pull your hands far apart. The ron-ron will spin. Quickly pump your hands back towards the button like you are clapping without your hands touching. Then pull your hands apart again. The string should twist and untwist. Continue to pump your hands in and out rapidly. The button will spin and start to whir, just like the ron-ron José played with.

Learn more about the Amazon

Books
Cherry, Lynn. *The Great Kapok Tree*. New York: Harcourt Brace and Company, 1990.

Jordan, Martin and Tanis. *Amazon Alphabet*. New York: Kingfisher Books, 1996.

Goodman, Susan E. *Bats, Bugs and Biodiversity: Adventures in the Amazonian Rainforest*. New York: Atheneum Books for Young Readers, 1995.

Van Laan, Nancy. *So Say the Little Monkeys*. New York: Atheneum Books for Young Readers, 1998. (A folktale from the Brazilian Amazon.)

Harris, Nicholas. *Into the Rainforest*. New York: TimeLife Books, 1996.

Morrison, Marion. *The Amazon Rainforest and Its People*. New York: Thomson Learning, 1993.

Pratt, Joy. *A Walk in the Rainforest*. Nevada City, Calif.: Dawn Publishing, 1992.

Willow, Diane and Laura Jacques. *At Home in the Rain Forest*. Watertown, Mass.: Charlesbridge Publishing, 1991.

Video
Amazon: Land of the Flooded Forest. National Geographic Video.

Web sites
Shedd Aquarium
www.sheddaquarium.org
Look for more information about Amazon animals.

Rainforest Alliance
www.rainforest-alliance.org/kids & teachers
Find information and activities for kids.

World Wildlife Fund
www.worldwildlifefund.org/global200/spaces.cfm
Click on "Featured Ecoregions" and scroll to "Flooded Forests of the Amazon."